W9-CLI-744

OKOMI
and the Tickling Game

Helen and
Clive Dorman

Illustrated by
Tony Hutchings

Dawn Publications
in association with The Jane Goodall Institute

It was a hot summer day.

Okomi and his mommy, Mama Du, were lying in the shade under a large, leafy tree.

They were having an afternoon nap.

It was so hot that Okomi didn't
want to wake up.

Mama Du saw
Okomi's little toes wiggling
as he stretched and yawned.

She was feeling playful.

She reached over and gently
tickled his foot!

Okomi quickly curled up
in a ball to try to hide his foot.

Then he laughed at his mommy.

Mama Du reached out
and tickled his foot again.

Okomi laughed and laughed.

Then he stretched out his leg
to wait for another tickle.

Mama Du tickled him again and again.

Then Mama Du
pretended she
was going
to tickle
Okomi's foot.

Instead she tickled
his tummy!

Okomi found this very funny.

"Ooo, Ooo, Ooo," he laughed as
he rolled over to escape from
his mommy's tickly hands.

Then he rolled back
to be tickled again.

After a while Mama Du was
too hot and tired to play.
She rolled onto her back to rest.
She stretched her arms out
above her head and gazed up
at the treetops.

Okomi looked at his mommy.
He was still playful.

Now it was his turn!

Very quietly,
his fingers moved
nearer and nearer to
Mama Du's underarm
and he tried to copy her.

She giggled and rolled over.

Okomi was very excited to
make his mommy happy.
He found the tickling game
funny, but also very tiring.

Soon he was ready to stop.

All the tickling
had made Okomi
and Mama Du
happy and hungry.

They had a big hug.

Then Mama Du lifted
Okomi onto her back
and they went
into the forest
to find some food.

The Work Of Jane Goodall

Jane with an orphan chimpanzee

For many years, Jane Goodall patiently watched chimpanzees in the African forest. She saw chimp babies play with their mothers and that chimpanzees have close family ties. She saw young chimps throw tantrums and have exciting learning adventures. She saw that the chimpanzee mother-infant relationship is virtually identical to its human counterpart.

Jane Goodall's research of more than 40 years showed how chimpanzees reason and solve problems, how they make tools and use them, and how they communicate. It revealed that they have a wide range of emotions. It showed that each of them has a unique, vivid personality. Indeed, their genetic makeup is closer to us than any other animal—with almost 99% identical DNA. Jane's revolutionary work bids us to look upon chimpanzees as non-human relatives.

Photo by Michael Neugebauer

Fanni and her baby, Fax.

Yet the plight of these "relatives" is desperate.
Their forests are being cut down. They are being hunted for food. Their numbers are dwindling drastically. And when chimpanzee mothers are killed, the orphaned babies—often taken to be sold illegally as pets—cannot be returned successfully to the wild.

When Jane realized that chimpanzees were becoming endangered, she began a worldwide effort on their behalf. She campaigns tirelessly, and established The Jane Goodall Institute. It has created sanctuaries for orphan chimpanzees. (You can help the orphans by "adopting a chimp.") It works to improve conditions in zoos and laboratories, and to halt deforestation and the bushmeat trade. The Institute also sponsors Roots & Shoots, a worldwide program for young people working to make a difference for animals, the environment and their communities. For more information contact The Jane Goodall Institute, P.O. Box 14890, Silver Spring, MD 20910, or call (301) 565-0086, or go to www.janegoodall.org.

DAWN PUBLICATIONS · A SHARING NATURE WITH CHILDREN BOOK

Part of the proceeds from the sale of this book supports the work of The Jane Goodall Institute's Tchimpounga Sanctuary in the Congo Republic. Dawn Publications is dedicated to inspiring in children a deeper understanding and appreciation for all life on Earth. To view our full list of titles, or to order, please visit our web site at www.dawnpub.com, or call 800-545-7475.

A Sharing Nature With Children Book

Published by arrangement with The Children's Project Ltd., P.O. Box 2, Richmond, TW10 7FL, U.K., and the Jane Goodall Institute Ltd., 15 Clarendon Park, Lymington, Hants SO41 8AX, U.K.

Library of Congress Cataloging-in-Publication Data

Dorman, Helen.
    Okomi : the tickling game / Helen and Clive Dorman ; illustrated by
Tony Hutchings. -- 1st ed.
            p. cm. -- (A sharing nature with children book)
Summary: Okomi, a young chimpanzee, plays a tickling game with his Mama
Du.
    ISBN 1-58469-046-1 (pbk.)
    1. Chimpanzees -- Juvenile fiction. [1. Chimpanzees--Fiction. 2.
Animals -- Infancy -- Fiction. 3. Tickling -- Fiction.] I. Dorman, Clive. II.
Hutchings, Tony, ill. III. Title. IV Series.
    PZ10.3.D7185 On 2003
    [E] -- dc21
                                2002015160

Dawn Publications
P.O. Box 2010
Nevada City, CA 95959
530-478-0111
nature@dawnpub.com
www.dawnpub.com

Printed in Korea

10 9 8 7 6 5 4 3 2 1
First Edition
Design and computer production by Andrea Miles